To Toby, for the inspiration

First edition 2016

Library of Congress Catalog Card Number pending
ISBN 978-0-7636-8093-0

16 17 18 19 20 21 CCP 10 9 8 7 6 5 4 3 2 1

Printed in Shenzhen, Guangdong, China

This book was typeset in Clue.
The illustrations were done in graphite and
watercolor wash and colored digitally.

Candlewick Press
99 Dover Street
Somerville, Massachusetts 02144

visit us at www.candlewick.com

Toby

Hazel Mitchell

CANDLEWICK PRESS

But I liked Toby.

We bought toys and treats and took Toby home.

He didn't want treats. And he didn't want to play.

That night he howled and howled . . .

and howled.

Woooo-woo.

I gave him my special rabbit.

And I slept right next to him.

When I brought him breakfast, he hid.

When will Toby play with me?

You'll have to be patient with him.

Then Toby had an accident.

Bad dog, Toby!

Hey, bud, come and clean up this mess!

It's time to do some training.

It didn't go too well.

He even thought the yard was scary!

Hiss!

So we tried again.

I'll be home soon!

I worried about Toby all day.

But he was waiting for me.

Want to play?

WOOF!

And then Dad showed me his glasses.

Maybe Toby isn't the right dog for us after all.

I promise he won't do it again.

We were going to have to work hard.

And we were going to have to work fast.

Sit!

Go fetch!

Lie down, Toby!

That was GREAT!

I knew Toby was the right dog for us.

But the next morning, Toby wasn't on my bed.

Dad . . .

Author's Note

The real Toby was rescued from a puppy mill in 2013 along with seven members of his poodle family, including his mother and grandmother. The dogs were taken to the Houlton Humane Society in Maine to await new homes. I offered to give a temporary foster home to Toby until he could be adopted by a permanent family. But he quickly stole my heart, and I decided to offer him a forever home and adopt him myself. At first Toby was very scared of his new world, then gradually he began to enjoy life. In the summer of 2014, he managed to get under a fence and ran off. The local community helped me search for him, walking miles along roads, trudging through woods, and kayaking on the river hoping to see Toby along the banks. Trained tracker dogs were brought in to try to pick up his scent. On the Internet, people from all over the world followed the search for Toby, checking Facebook each day for news. Then, after eight long days lost in the countryside, Toby found his own way back home, and everyone breathed a sigh of relief—including Toby! His favorite things are playing with his stuffed toys, getting treats, chasing the cat, and finding my shoes.

— Hazel & Toby